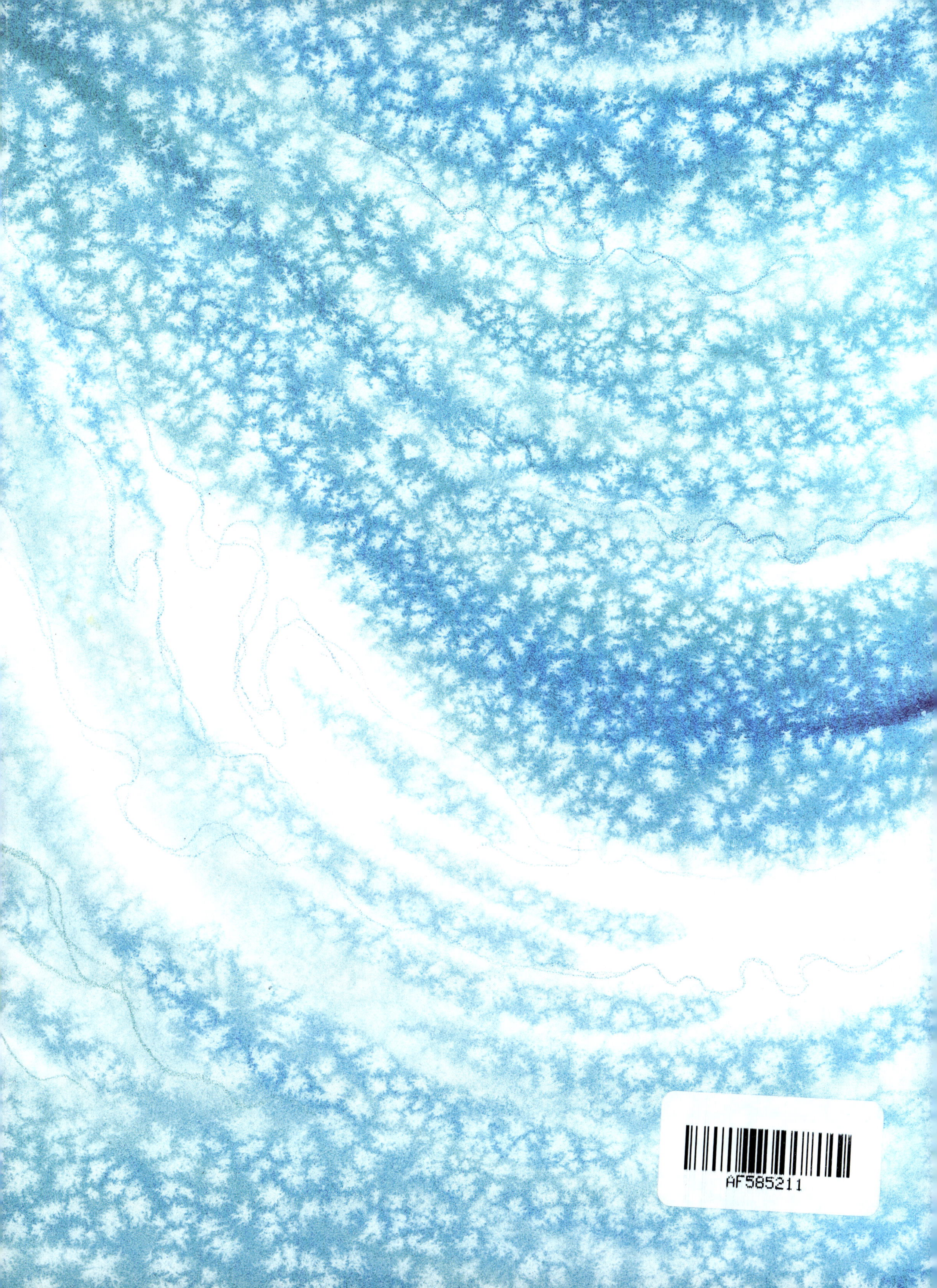
AF585211

FLOAT OR SINK?

Kylie Covark   Andrew Plant

FORD ST

For Mikey, who lifts everybody up – KC

For our wonderful teachers,
who, during the 2020 COVID-19 pandemic,
kept our children afloat – AP

First published by Ford Street Publishing, Melbourne, Victoria, Australia

2 4 6 8 10 9 7 5 3 1

ISBN: 9781 925804 614 (hardcover)
ISBN: 9781925804621 (paperback)

Ford Street website: www.fordstreetpublishing.com
First published 2021

A catalogue record for this book is available from the National Library of Australia

Design & layout: Cathy Larsen Design

Printed in China by Tingleman Pty Ltd

There's a stick in a creek,
bobbing along,
rolling on,
light but strong.

What do you think?

Float...

or sink?

Ladybug Red
flips onto her head,
a dangerous trick
on top of a stick.

And the stick bobs along,
it's light but it's strong.

What do you think?

Float...

Or sink?

Sir Fergal McFlea
dreams of the sea,
on top of the stick
where the bug does a trick.

And the stick bobs along,
it's light but it's strong.

What do you think?

Float...

Or sink?

Lord Fly rests his wings
and quietly sings,
next to the flea
who dreams of the sea,
on top of the stick
where the bug does a trick.

And the stick bobs along,
it's light but it's strong.

What do you think?

Float...

Or sink?

On springs Dame Gnat
who is keen for a chat,
as the fly rests his wings
and quietly sings,
next to the flea
who dreams of the sea,
on top of the stick
where the bug does a trick.

And the stick bobs along,
it's light but it's strong.

What do you think?

Float...

Or sink?

Countess von Slug
gives the gnat a big hug,
as the fly rests his wings
and quietly sings,
next to the flea
who dreams of the sea,
on top of the stick
where the bug does a trick.

And the stick bobs along,
it's light but it's strong.

What do you think?

Float...

Or sink?

Last comes Queen Quack
on the hunt for a snack,
spies the gnat and the slug
still lost in their hug,
the soft-singing fly
with his eyes to the sky,
and the fanciful flea
who scans for the sea –
all on the stick
where the bug does her trick.

And the stick bobs along,
it's light but it's strong.

What do you think?

Float...

Or sink?

Greedy Queen Quack
swoops in for a snack,
she misses her mark
and lands on her back.

And the stick bobs along,
it's light but it's strong.

What do you think?

Float...
or sink?